The diary of
A YOUNG TUDOR
LADY-IN-WAITING

Editor Louisa Sladen
Editor-in-Chief John C. Miles
Designer Jason Billin / Billin Design Solutions
Art Director Jonathan Hair

© 2000 Franklin Watts

First published in 2000
by Franklin Watts
96 Leonard Street
London
EC2A 4XD

Franklin Watts Australia
14 Mars Road
Lane Cove
NSW 2066

ISBN 0 7496 3662 9 (hbk)
0 7496 3943 1 (pbk)

Dewey classification: 942.05

A CIP catalogue record for this book is available
from the British Library.

Printed in Great Britain

The diary of
A YOUNG TUDOR LADY-IN-WAITING

by Natalie Grice

Illustrated by Brian Duggan

FRANKLIN WATTS

NEW YORK • LONDON • SYDNEY

FEBRUARY 7, 1585

I am so excited I can barely hold my quill.
Dick has just arrived from London with a letter
to Mother from Aunt Catherine. The Queen has
agreed to receive me at court. She told Aunt that
I may come immediately. I can't believe it.
At last I'm going to get to see more of the world
than boring old Huntsdon. Thank you, Queen
Elizabeth, thank you from the bottom of
my heart.

Mother told me I would have to have new
clothes before I could go, because I would be a
disgrace to the whole family if I went in the
dresses I had "ruined" as she put it. Honestly,
you'd think it was my fault it rains in England.
Is it so wrong to want to be outdoors rather
than sitting next to the fire all day, moaning
about being cold? Thank goodness Father and
John let me go out riding on Star with them as
much as they do. I'd go wild if I was cooped up
indoors all the time.

Of course, that was the first thing Mother

4

started lecturing me about. "When you're at court, Rebecca, you'll have to do exactly as you're told. You'll learn to sit still like a good, obedient lady, and not go dashing around the place as if you were possessed by a demon."

I nearly burst trying not to laugh when Mother said that! I have to admit, it is one of the things I'm a bit worried about. But everybody says that the court is a whirl of activity, with dancing and masques every night. How can you be sitting still if so much is happening? I think Mother is just trying to frighten me.

⊶⟨▭▭▭⟩◉◉⟨▭▭▭⟩⊷

The only time I don't mind sitting in the house is when I'm playing the virginals. The music seems to carry me away to a different place and I don't notice where I am. It will be so wonderful to hear all the music and join in the dancing at court.

I'm going to London. London, London, London! Aunt Catherine said in the letter that I will join the court at Whitehall if I arrive before April. Then she expects the Queen to move to Greenwich. It's going to be funny being with my aunt.

She's father's half-sister and is nearly thirty years younger than him. She's not married yet either.

I'll have weeks of sewing to do now, I suppose. That's the worst thing about being a poor gentlewoman. You have these huge dresses which you have to wear (according to Mother anyway), and no money to pay seamstresses. At least the peasants only have plain clothes to make. The last time Mother complained about the state of my dress, I told her I would wear a peasant's dress instead. She nearly dropped dead from shock. Why are clothes so important? I just do not understand. Perhaps I will when I get to court …

MARCH 2, 1585

This is my third night on the road. I didn't have the energy to write before now. I did not realise how tiring travelling all day could be. Even my sturdy mare Star seemed worn out by dusk. And,

I have to be honest, I was too upset to write the first two nights. I never thought I would miss Huntsdon so much. The inns we have been staying at seem so grimy and dark in comparison.

―――――――――

But Father has been cheering me up no end. He keeps telling me stories of when he was in London when King Henry was alive and some of the hunts and dances he attended. That was before Grandfather fell out of favour with the King, of course, and he had to leave court quickly. Father has never spoken about it to me; I've always had to rely on John for information. But that's why our family is so poor now, because the King took away a large chunk of our land and gave it to horrible Sir William Bluck of Boundstead. If Father hadn't already been married to Mother, he would have been practically penniless. It was a good thing she had a fairly large dowry. Not that it lasted for ever.

All this keeping up appearances that Mother keeps going on about – meaning having fancy clothes and sending expensive presents to court every Christmas – has cost Father a fortune. I don't know why he goes along with it. But I did hear Mother saying to him the night before we left, "It's starting to pay off, Robert. As long as Rebecca catches the right one, we'll be all right." Now what does she mean by that?

March 5, 1585

London! It's like another world. So many houses, so many people, so much life! Oh, thank you, Lord, for bringing me here. I feel as if I was born to live here.

⚬══╍╍╍OO╍╍╍══⚬

We arrived at a friend of Father's today. We are staying here until Aunt Catherine comes to take me to court in two days' time. Mr de Courcey, Father's friend, is not short of a florin or two. He is a merchant who deals in cloth and materials. All his servants wear rich velvet clothes and have his family crest stitched on them. The goblets they used at dinner today – an ordinary day, not a feast day or a holy day – are made of silver, with gold edgings – no pewter for the de Courceys! We drank wine too, not ale. I tell you, this is living grandly. Dining at court could surely not be more fine.

March 6, 1585

Father took me out today to show me the city.
We rode across London Bridge to Southwark.
The bridge is amazing. It has houses built up on
both sides which look from a distance as if they
are floating in the air. But the best is the river. Its
flowing currents carry thousands of barges and
ships busily boating up and down, and back and
forth from bank to bank. I could have stayed all
day watching it.

Father said we had to go and give thanks for
my good fortune, as he put it. We rode down
East Cheap and Watling Street, and there in front
of me was the most incredible sight yet – stone
tracery, reaching endlessly up into the sky. As we
got nearer, my neck craned back until my mouth
was wide open. It was St Paul's Cathedral, the
greatest house of worship in all England.

I felt like an ant going into the cathedral.
That was the easiest prayer I ever said. For once,
I really am thankful for all the blessings I have
received.

MARCH 7, 1585

I have met the Queen of England. Her gracious Majesty, Elizabeth the First, Gloriana, the Virgin Queen. And I can say this certainly (and pray nobody ever reads this diary) – she is absolutely terrifying.

Catherine took me into the court room which was buzzing with the chatter of milling courtiers. I was dazzled by their brightness. Everyone I looked at glowed with strong, brilliant colours. Not just their clothes – the men's beards and hair were glowing too! They were dyed orange or purple or yellow, to match the garments they wore. For all my nerves, I just stared for a moment. I had never seen anything so bizarre. They looked like exotic birds.

A group of these parrot-like creatures were grouped together. As we approached, some of them moved back and I saw her for the first time – Elizabeth! She was wearing a pure white velvet dress, covered in tiny pearls.

On her head was a striking red wig, more vibrant than any other in the room. Her skin was paler than the pearls. Her eyebrows arched high above her brown eyes, making her look as if she was constantly questioning whoever spoke. She had lots of red make-up on her cheeks, which looked strange against her white face.

The Queen was talking to one young man who was listening attentively to her. Catherine waited for her to finish, then politely cleared her throat. I stood hesitantly behind her, half-hiding.

The Queen looked up after a moment. "Yes, Mistress Swann, what is it?"

"If you please, ma'am, I would like to present my niece, Rebecca Swann. Your Majesty was so kind as to –"

"Yes, yes," Elizabeth interrupted sharply. I flinched inside. "Bring her forward."

Catherine took my hand and swept me forward. Raising her voice slightly, to catch the attention of the gathered courtiers, she said, "Your Majesty, here is Rebecca Swann, of Huntsdon in Gloucestershire."

She squeezed my hand to give me my cue. I kicked my skirt back and curtsied as low as I could without falling over – it really isn't one of my best skills – and waited for the Queen to speak.

"You are welcome to my court," she said. I took that as a sign that I could straighten up. Good thing too. My legs were trembling. She paused.

I took a breath. "I thank Your Majesty for the kindness you are showing me. I bring greetings and a token of esteem from my father and mother, Walter and Mary Swann." I took out a velvet pouch and carefully handed it to her.

She slipped the bracelet out, glanced swiftly at it, and said, "A pretty trinket. Thank you most kindly. Catherine, you may take her to the ladies' chambers." And with that she turned back to the young man. We turned and started for the door.

Just as I was thinking, What a lovely lady, I don't know where these nasty stories about her come from, the fiercest voice I have ever heard in my entire life screeched, "What is she doing here?"

I froze. Had she suddenly had a change of heart? Then I didn't have time to think because Catherine pushed me hard back against the wall as the Queen swept past us. For somebody of fifty-two, she is very fleet and agile.

My first thought was relief. It wasn't me she was after. A young woman with black hair and dark blue eyes (which looked raw from crying) had entered the room. As the Queen approached, she dropped to her knees and spread her arms out in a pleading manner.

"Please, Your Majesty, please have mercy and let him go," she cried. "Have I not been a good and faithful servant to you? Please do not reward me in this way. Please –"

"Silence!" bellowed the Queen. "I ordered you to leave. How dare you disobey me. Now leave or you shall join your so-called husband."

"But –"

The Queen lifted her hand and slapped the woman across the face. "I said SILENCE!"

The woman, tears running down her face, picked up her skirts and ran from the court room. The courtiers immediately surrounded the Queen, and I could hear snippets of conversation: "Terrible cheek," "What a performance," and, here and there the odd quiet murmur of "Poor girl." Catherine and I slipped quietly out.

Alas, my candle is running out. I shall continue the story tomorrow.

MARCH 8, 1585

I have woken up before the other girls so I can finish yesterday's entry. Where was I? Catherine didn't say anything to me on the way to the bedchambers, and I was too stunned to ask any questions. She showed me where I would be sleeping. By the way, I'm sharing a room with four other young ladies-in-waiting and one more mature one who is there to "regulate our conduct", as Catherine put it. Once I had seen the ways in and out of the Queen's bedchamber and where the privy was, she took me aside into a window seat to show me the view of the Thames.

But once we were sitting, she said, in a lowered voice, "I don't know how much your mother has told you about the Queen. I want to warn you, Rebecca, to stop you having a fate like Anna's, that woman you just saw."

"What did she do?" I asked, thinking she must have committed a terrible crime to provoke the Queen so much.

"She got married," answered my aunt.

"Got married?" I repeated. "What's so terrible about that? I thought everybody was supposed to get married, except priests."

"If you are one of the Queen's ladies or courtiers, you must have her permission to marry," explained Catherine. "Anna married a courtier, Sir Richard Holdenby, even though she knew the Queen didn't approve. As soon as she found out, she sent Sir Richard to the Marshalsea Prison and banished Anna from the court."

"How long will he be in prison for?" I asked.

Catherine shrugged and looked out of the window. "As long as the Queen feels like keeping him there. Anna was foolish today. She should just have gone away quietly for a month or two and let Sir Richard's friends persuade the Queen to release him. The Queen likes him really. That's one of the reasons she didn't want him to get married. She wanted all his attention for herself."

It all seemed very complicated to me. Maybe I'd understand more once I got used to life here. Catherine turned to me again. "So what I want you to learn is this, Rebecca. Don't disobey the Queen – and don't fall in love with the wrong person."

I laughed. "Fall in love? At my age?"

"That's a good girl," she said. "It will be much easier to find you a husband with an attitude like that."

I stared at her. "What do you mean, find me a husband? I'm not getting married. I'm only fifteen."

Now it was her turn to stare at me. "Hasn't your mother told you?" She sighed. " Oh dear, I was afraid of something like this. Rebecca, you haven't mixed much in society because of your father's situation. You may not be aware of how things work. Your parents have sent you here because they want you to find a rich husband who will help restore your family's fortunes. This is your duty."

"But – but I don't want to!" I burst out. "I want to dance and hunt and do all the things I've heard so much about. I don't want to get married!"

"Whether you want to or not is not important. It's whether you will be offered marriage by a suitable man. You don't have a large marriage portion, and as many men come to court looking for rich wives as do women looking for rich husbands. It will not be your decision. If somebody asks for your hand, it will be for your parents to say yes or no, not you. You must remember that, Rebecca."

I was too miserable to answer. I had thought court would be an answer to my prayers. It seemed I had celebrated too soon.

May 2, 1585: Greenwich

We have been at Greenwich Palace for nearly three weeks. I must say, it was a relief to leave Whitehall. The court had been staying there for nearly five months and it smelt horrible. There were chewed bones and dropped bits of rotten fruit trodden into the rushes on the floor, and so many rats everywhere.

Here in Greenwich it is very pleasant. I have made friends with most of the youngest maids of honour. There is Lady Sarah Owen, who comes from Pembrokeshire all the way in the west of Wales, Grace Markham, who hardly says a word but works very hard at her lute, and the twin sisters, Ladies Dorothea and Laetitia D'Arcy, or Dotty and Letty as we call them when we're alone. But my favourite is Frances Highwater from Bath. We laugh at the same things and have lots in common. We've already become good friends.

I told Frances what Catherine said about getting married. She told me not to worry, because the Queen didn't like anybody paying attention to her young maids of honour. So I should be safe until I'm a bit older.

Lady Dorothea
D'Arcy

Lady Laetitia
D'Arcy

Grace Markham

Lady Sarah Owen

Frances Highwater

I have become used to the duties expected of me. We rise with the Queen at about six. We sit in her bedchamber while her maids dress her and powder her face. I have noticed that somebody must always say how well she looks, or how her dress becomes her. We all attend morning prayers. Then it is time for breakfast, which the Queen sometimes eats in her chamber while consulting with one of her ministers. Most of the mornings are spent either in the court room or the Queen's privy chamber, depending on whether she feels like having privacy or not. We play cards with her and sometimes one of the ladies will play music or sing to her. Occasionally she will dismiss us while she speaks in private with others, but usually at least one of the older ladies stays with her. Then after lunch, around eleven, she may take the air in the gardens. We accompany her there, which I like. When we have dinner depends on if there is entertainment planned for the evening.

Sometimes we are in bed by eight, sometimes by twelve, once not until three in the morning. But the Queen never appears fatigued. She is indeed a very energetic woman.

I've seen some sights, I must say. Last week, ambassadors from Holland came for an audience with the Queen and they were treated to the most lavish banquet I've ever seen.

The banqueting hall was glowing with thousands of candles and lanterns, and draped in rich tapestries. Catherine was seated next to me and she pointed out people I have heard lots of tales about: the Queen's favourite, the Earl of Leicester, whom everybody thought she was going to marry when she was younger; William Cecil, the royal secretary; the Earl of Essex, Robert Devereux, and his beautiful sister, Lady Penelope Rich. I also met Catherine's suitor, John Greene, whom she is going to marry this summer. We had fourteen courses at that feast – I thought I was going to explode before it was over, and I only nibbled a little of each course. But the best of all came after the feast. Ten of the senior ladies-in-waiting entertained us with a masque they had devised about the goddess Diana. The costumes they were wearing were marvellous. They had shimmering veils, and silvery bows. All of them had cleverly painted masks to represent different characters. They showed Diana and her handmaidens living free and avoiding the world of men. I was spellbound. The women were truly goddesses in my eyes. I want to be like them. I am determined to be in a masque before long.

MAY 25, 1585

I played the virginals for the first time today since I left home. There is an instrument in the court room but I haven't had the chance to play on it yet. So many of the other ladies use it. This morning, though, everybody was out taking the air with the Queen. So I saw my chance and slipped into the empty court room.

It was lovely to be able to play again. I completely forgot where I was. In fact I was so lost in the music, I started singing.

Then, at the end of my fourth song, somebody behind me started clapping. I jumped off the stool as if I'd been shot by a musket. A young man just a few years older than me was standing at the back of the room, leaning on the door. He was tall and slim, with chestnut hair that curled to his shoulders and the lightest blue eyes I have ever seen. He was wearing a dark blue cloak which fell to his knees, fastened at the breast with a sparkling brooch.

He said quickly but gently, "No, please don't stop. I'm sorry I disturbed you. I just couldn't help myself, my lady."

I felt unusually tongue-tied – very unlike my normal, outspoken self. After an awkward pause,

I said, "I am no lady, sir. My name is simply Rebecca Swann."

He gave me a little smile. "Good day, simply Rebecca Swann."

For no reason at all, I blushed as he said my name. His smile grew bigger and he took a few steps into the room. "I haven't seen you at court before. You are one of Her Majesty's new ladies, I presume."

"Yes," I said, hoping my cheeks had cooled a little.

"The Queen must be delighted to have such a clever performer to entertain her," he said, advancing a few more steps.

"Oh – " I stammered, "I – I don't –"
What was wrong with me? I never stammered. I tried again. "I haven't played for her. The other ladies – "

" – do not play half as well as you," he interrupted. "You should play for her. She will be very pleased, and believe me, anything that pleases her is good news."

In the distance, a man's voice called something. My strange new friend stuck his head out of the door and called, "I'm coming."

He looked back at me. "I'm afraid I have to go. It was nice to meet you, Mistress Swann. I hope to see you again some day."

It seemed an odd thing to say. If he was at court, I'd probably see him most days, wouldn't I?

He bowed and turned to go.

"Wait," I said, rather more sharply than I intended. "I don't know your name, sir."

He grinned. "It's Will Devine – and I am not a sir either – but I will be one day, I promise you that."

And with that he ran out of the room.

MAY 26, 1585

I asked Catherine about Will Devine today. I didn't tell her about meeting him – I didn't tell anybody about that – I just said that his name was mentioned in passing. What she told me has made me feel sad.

He is leaving England as part of an expedition to the Spanish Main, and will not be back for many months, maybe years. He, like me, is from a poor but good family. His father died when he was a boy and he has lived as a ward in

William Cecil's house. Catherine says he has no prospects except those he makes for himself.

I don't know why I asked about him. I only met him for two minutes after all. And now it looks like I may never meet him again. So why can't I stop thinking about him?

JANUARY 8, 1586: RICHMOND

I have been so busy learning how to be a maid of honour and not to put a foot wrong that I have been quite unable to write in my diary these eight months! I must do better in future.

The threat of the plague in London is finally over. Catherine and John have a house near the Tower and she told me they saw as many as twenty bodies taken away on the carts one day. That was before they also came to Richmond to escape it. She told me she was terrified that they had caught the plague and kept checking for

signs of it every few hours. It's not so bad for the gentry who can afford to leave the city. But what about the common people of London? They can't run to the country. It must be even more frightening for them.

The court is getting ready to celebrate the anniversary of Elizabeth's coronation, and, at last, I have the chance to take part. Lady Fitzwilliam, one of the senior ladies, was talking to Catherine about the masque they are thinking of doing. She said they need a quantity of ostrich feathers. She mentioned that nobody could think where to get any, because their supplier had died of the pestilence.

Quick as a flash, I remembered that Father's friend Mr de Courcey dealt in adornments, and saw my opportunity. I said, " I know where to get feathers, my lady."

I thought she was going to scold me for being forward, but she only said, "Wonderful. Then I shall put you in charge of the feathers, Mistress Swann."

But I wanted more than that. So I screwed up my courage and said, "Please, my lady, could I be in the masque? I have dreamed of being in one ever since I saw the masque of Diana. It was so wonderful."

Lady Fitzwilliam smiled. "That was my idea," she said. (I knew it was – I also knew the Queen wasn't the only person around the court who liked to be flattered.) "I'm glad you enjoyed it. Well, as Lady Constance has been taken sick, we are short by one performer. It seems a fair reward for your work with the feathers. Yes, you may join us."

I was in seventh heaven. "Thank you so much. I won't let you down."

I have written to Mr de Courcey placing the order for a large batch of ostrich feathers. When they arrive, I am going to make them into headdresses for all the masquers. For the first time, I am glad of all the sewing I've had to do over the years. I have a plan for what to do with them.

JANUARY 9, 1586

I had such a funny dream last night. I dreamt that Will Devine was playing the virginals while I danced on a bed of ostrich feathers. Then the peacocks on the tapestries came to life and started chasing me. All the time I was getting further and further away from Will and the music. He was playing the tune I had been playing when we met.

Even though it is over half a year since we met, I still think about him. I just don't understand why.

JANUARY 15, 1586
ANNIVERSARY OF THE CORONATION

Oh what a day, what a day! I could die tonight and be happy. I am the toast of the court. Let me record this day for history's sake. Luckily I am alone tonight, so I have time to write everything down in my diary.

The morning started with a grand procession up to the City of London. Country and city folks lined the route to get a glimpse of the Queen. For once she was not wearing white or black but had on a dazzling dress of red velvet with fine silver netting woven over the velvet. She also wore a ruby and diamond necklace and tiara and a massive high collar of cloth-of-silver framing her face. She did look impressive. She rode in an open carriage despite the cold and waved and shouted to her subjects who seemed delighted with her friendly behaviour. I wondered if they would be so delighted if they saw her having one of her tantrums.

We crossed the river at Kingston and made our way up towards Westminster Abbey. The sun was shining brightly and it was amazingly warm for this time of year. I heard the Queen say loudly to the Earl of Essex, who was riding close to her carriage, "Even the sun obeys the royal command. I told him to shine, and he does."

Frances, who was riding next to me, choked back a laugh and turned it into a cough. I had to do the same. Frances is terrible like that. I always know when the Queen says something outrageous that she will find it as funny as I do. The trouble is, she can't stop herself laughing, and it makes me laugh too. One of these days, we're going to get ourselves in real trouble. If the Queen heard us we would face her wrath.

Where was I? Oh yes. Well, when we arrived at Westminster I didn't hear a word of the service because I was too busy worrying about the headdresses I'd made. Nobody had seen them yet, not even Lady Fitzwilliam, and I was afraid she might not like them.

I needn't have worried. Lady Fitzwilliam was far too occupied with another problem when I went to take the headdresses to her. Lady Rachel, who was supposed to be playing and singing for the Queen after the masque, had come down with the same illness as Lady Constance, griping in the guts, and couldn't even speak, let alone sing.

I gave a delicate cough. "My lady, if I might make a suggestion …"

I couldn't tell you who was at dinner, what we ate, what we drank, who I spoke to – all I could think about was what was coming after. When the sweet ginger was being served, Lady Fitzwilliam made a gesture to those of us performing, and we quietly slipped away from our tables. There was so much bustle and noise, from the diners and the musicians playing in the corner, that no one noticed us go.

In our chambers, we took our outer dresses off and slipped on our costumes made for the masque. Each of the masquers put on her headdress and I was absolutely delighted – they looked even better than I had imagined.

We made our way back to the dining hall, and waited at the door while the steward announced our names. I could see that tables had been cleared to give us room. I started to feel queasy. My hands and feet turned cold as ice. There were lots of very important men and women in that room. What if I made a complete fool of myself? I would have to leave court, disgraced, my name would be the laughing stock of London . . .

The Master of Ceremonies spoke. "If it please Your Majesty and this court, the ladies of honour humbly present for your entertainment the masque, Glory of Anglia."

We walked into the room in a circle, with Lady Fitzwilliam hidden in the centre. At a signal, the lamps in the hall were swiftly put out. People gasped.

Lady Rosamund, to my left, started to speak. "Anglia reached a dark and worrying night. All was black and there was no light."

A few lamps were relit. Eleven of us in the circle were bent forward, so that our headdresses touched.

Rosamund continued, "Then out of the darkness came new hope. A star arose and shone brightly, sending back the shadows."

We started to sink to our knees. Lady Fitzwilliam, who had been crouched low in the centre of the circle, straightened up. Her headdress was twice as magnificent as the others I had made. A steward handed her a burning lamp, which she held high above her head.

She spoke again with great solemnity. "I am Glory, the saviour of Anglia. I have come to lead my people forward to a new age of peace, happiness and godliness."

We all shouted, "Three cheers for Glory of Anglia."

Everybody in the court joined in. Of course they realised it was Elizabeth we were really cheering. I stole a quick glance at the Queen. She was smiling and nodding her head to acknowledge the cheers.

We continued with our masque, which showed Glory accepting the sceptre of office, and the adoration of her "subjects". The Queen applauded very energetically at the end. That showed that the masque had been a great success.

But now it was my moment of triumph – or failure. Two servants brought the virginals to the centre of the room and I sat down at the keyboard. I could hear a surprised murmur run around the court. It wasn't usual for somebody of my age to perform to such a big audience.

I sang a song which had been composed not long after Elizabeth's coronation. It spoke of the relief the people of England felt to have her on the throne after the horrors of her sister Mary's reign. We all knew this was a favourite theme of the Queen's.

At the end, there was silence as everybody waited for the Queen's reaction. If she didn't like my performance, no one else would dare approve it. I kept my eyes glued to my fingers.

The Queen got to her feet. Everybody

watched quietly. She got down off the raised platform she was sitting on and approached me.

"Well, Mistress Swann, I am quite cross with you –" She paused.

Oh no. Somehow, I had managed to offend her, it seemed. I waited for her anger to break.

"Yes, I am quite cross with you", she repeated, "for hiding your talent from your Queen until now. A sweeter voice I have yet to hear. Well done." And she started clapping.

Well, there was uproar. All the courtiers outdid each other to see who could clap louder. There were shouts of "Bravo" and "Encore".

I played again, to the same response. At the dancing afterwards, I had five men asking to be my partner at every dance. It seems that suddenly I am someone who matters at court, and I am very pleased.

FEBRUARY 10, 1587: WESTMINSTER

A year has passed, and Mary Stuart, Queen of Scots, is dead. Queen Elizabeth finally signed her death warrant ten days ago. There has been so much talk ever since Mary's trial for treason against Elizabeth last year. It seemed as if the Queen would never agree to sentence her cousin to death, but she has done it.

I still don't really understand what it is all about. As far as I can see, Mary was a threat to Elizabeth because she was a Catholic. Catholics in England wanted her to be the ruler of England instead of Elizabeth. Mary was the heir to the English throne, but now King James of Scotland, her son, will become King when Queen Elizabeth dies. Nobody seems to think he will threaten Queen Elizabeth. I suppose he's much younger so he is prepared to wait for the English throne, and he's got his own kingdom of Scotland already.

It is such a strange situation. Queen Mary was a prisoner in England for so many years.

Queen Elizabeth was supposed to be offering her protection after she fled to England when she was turned off the Scottish throne because people said she had had her husband murdered. But everybody knew that Elizabeth wanted to keep an eye on her.

The thing that I think is the most horrible is that King James didn't try to help his mother in any way. I know he hadn't seen her since he was a child, but she was still his mother. It goes against God to go against your parents. At least, that's what Mother was always telling me when I was at home. She and I don't see eye to eye on many things, but I would defend her to the death if she was in danger.

People in court are divided about this. Many seem to think Mary should have been executed years ago. Others think this will be an excuse for Catholics in Spain and France to declare war on England.

Frances was very upset by it, as some of her family are Catholics. She said because of the treason trial, all Catholics will be persecuted. But I remember my father saying that Protestants were persecuted when the old Queen Mary, who was a Catholic, was on the throne. He says that things are much better under Elizabeth because she leaves people alone to worship how they please, as long as they don't make a big thing of it.

I find it all very confusing. I go to church and

don't think much about who is supposed to be the head of it, the Queen or the Pope. I just think people should try and get on with each other. It seems to be all to do with politics and power rather than worshipping God. But I would not say so to anyone – except this diary. The Queen is the head of the Protestant religion here in England. So no word must be said against the church.

MARCH 5, 1587

It is absolutely horrible at court. Everybody is in fear of what the Queen will do next. She has sent Sir William Davison to the Tower of London. All he did was deliver Mary's death warrant to her gaolers. Nobody knows what is going to happen to him. People are tiptoeing around as if they are walking on eggshells. Suddenly, the little jokes and tricks that go on behind the Queen's back have stopped. I am, I must admit, quite scared. I would rather be anywhere than here right now.

One of the ladies whispered to me that the Queen is afraid of the prophecies that say she will die next because she dared to take another Queen's life. A Jesuit priest who was found hiding in a house in London is to be hanged tomorrow. To my horror, we have all been ordered to accompany the Queen to Tower Hill to watch it.

MARCH 6, 1587

Tower Hill is right outside the Tower of London, where Elizabeth herself was held for some time when her sister Queen Mary was on the throne. We had arrived early in the morning, and were seated on a raised stage, to give the Queen an uninterrupted view.

I had never been to an execution before today. I have seen bodies hanging on gibbets, and I once saw a man killed by falling from a runaway horse. But I'd never seen so many people gathered to deliberately watch another man die.

Catherine told me that most of the people who were executed at Tower Hill were nobles or gentlemen and women. They were allowed to die by beheading. But this Jesuit priest was not noble, and he was going to be hanged, drawn and quartered like a traitor.

There must have been thousands of people on Tower Hill. The gallows were prepared, with the noose already dangling from them and the fire alight to burn parts of the Jesuit's body. I could hear lots of people in the crowd muttering prayers. Some seemed to be looking forward to the execution, but there were also a lot of grim faces.

At exactly ten o'clock, a man dressed simply in long dark robes was led through the crowd towards the scaffold. He climbed up the stairs, followed by the hangman who had a hood over his face. A Protestant priest followed and started saying some prayers, but the Jesuit waved him away.

The official who was conducting the execution read out the charges of treason against the Jesuit and the sentence. Then he asked the priest if he had anything to say.

The man turned to the crowd. His face looked calm. "If following the one true Christian faith is a crime, then I am guilty. If wishing to restore this faith to England is a crime, I am guilty twice. As I go willingly to meet God, I ask him in the name of the Catholic religion to guide and bless Queen Elizabeth. God save the Queen and England!"

There was a mixed reaction from the crowd. Some people booed at the mention of Catholicism. Some cheered – although whether for the priest, or for the Queen's name, it was difficult to say.

The hangman stood the priest on a stool, and placed the noose around his neck. I couldn't look. But I didn't want to be accused of sympathising with a traitor. So I pretended to be praying, which was a way of closing my eyes without drawing attention to myself.

First I heard the stool being pushed away, and there was the sound of a rope creaking. After only thirty seconds I heard the executioner cut the priest down, still very much alive, and the Jesuit's agonised groans of pain as his private parts were hacked off and his guts ripped out and thrown into the fire. I felt very sick and didn't open my eyes until after the butcher had announced "Behold the heart of a traitor!" and showed it to the eager crowd. I was so glad I hadn't seen his death. But I heard it – and it was very dreadful.

The Queen got up and swept off the platform. I've never seen her look so stony faced. Whatever will happen next?

July 1, 1588: Greenwich

The Spanish are coming to invade England! We've been expecting it since spring, but last night the Queen had a report that a fleet of Spanish ships called the Armada have been spotted off the coast of Plymouth.

Once again, it's madness here. The Earl of Leicester has been sent to Tilbury (further down the Thames) to oversee the preparations for war on land, if it comes to that. The cowards in the court are saying we will all be tortured and killed by the Spaniards.

Fiddle. Our ships are the best in the world. Admiral Sir Francis Drake has beaten Spanish sailors all round the world. The Queen's not running around moaning. Neither will I!

August 10, 1588

There has been fighting in the English Channel. So far, the reports seem to be good, but it's difficult to know the truth. A messenger this morning said that a storm has driven the Armada along the east coast of England.

The Queen is going to visit the troops at Tilbury. Some of the court are attending her, but I'm not, because I've got a nasty cold and the Queen doesn't like anyone who's ill to be near her.

Frances has been away for a few weeks visiting her home. Her mother was sick and they thought she might die, but I had a letter from her yesterday saying she had recovered. I'm looking forward to Frances coming back. She's my best friend, and I miss her.

AUGUST 15, 1588

Reports of the Queen's speech to the soldiers have come back to the palace. Apparently, she finished with this: "I know I have the body of a weak and feeble woman, but I have the heart and stomach of a king, and a King of England too. I myself will take up arms, I myself will be your general, judge and rewarder of every one of your virtues in the field."

Well, I'd get up and fight for her too if I could! God and St George for England! Hurrah for Queen Elizabeth!

AUGUST 29, 1588

Lord Dudley, the Earl of Leicester, is dead. The Queen is beside herself with grief. I can't see that anybody else is grief-stricken. Nobody seemed to like him very much except Her Majesty.

His step-son, the Earl of Essex, has already taken over Leicester's apartment at the court. He is getting all the attention now. All the people who were nice to Leicester to his face and horrible behind his back are doing just the same to Essex. At this time I really don't like living here.

SEPTEMBER 20, 1588

The Armada was soundly beaten. Their ships sailed all the way up the coast of England and round the top of Scotland, and a lot of them landed in Ireland. I think they were hoping to get help from the Irish, because they are Catholics too. But lots of the Spanish sailors were killed by English troops in Ireland.

It is said that only a third of the original Armada made it back to Spain. That'll teach them to try and defeat Queen Elizabeth. She's invincible.

OCTOBER 20, 1589: GREENWICH

Will Devine is back at court. I saw him this
morning when we accompanied Queen
Elizabeth to morning worship. He was sitting in
the back of the church. He got up, as everyone
does, when the Queen entered the room. I was
actually carrying her Bible, and I nearly dropped
it when I saw him. Good thing I didn't.

He bowed as the Queen passed. But when he
saw me as he stood up, he gave me a big grin.
I grinned back. It's not very ladylike to grin, but
I didn't care. I was so pleased to see him alive
and well. He looks just the same, except his face
is a darker colour, because of the sun no doubt.

Well, I couldn't for one moment concentrate
on what the priest was saying in the service.
I was dying to talk to him, and ask him
questions about the places he has seen in the
last two years. I can't fathom what it must be
like to sail over the oceans and not see land for
weeks or months at a time.

After the service, I had to escort the Queen

back to the privy chamber and attend her for half an hour. Then she decided she needed to see Secretary Cecil immediately, and sent me to fetch him.

As I was going towards Cecil's chambers, I heard somebody calling my name. I turned round to see Will running along the passage after me. He caught up with me and gave a quick bow.

"Mistress Swann, well met," he said. "How are you? Not that I need to ask – you look as well as ever. It seems only yesterday I heard you singing in the court room."

"I'm very well, thank you, Mr Devine. I'm glad to see you survived your journeys at sea."

He gave me that grin again. "Only just. I'd be happy to tell you about my travels. Perhaps we could go for a ride this afternoon?"

Now that was the annoying thing about being at court. If you were a young unmarried woman, you couldn't just go off on your own with a man – it would cause scandalous talk. However, I knew there was a hunting party going out tomorrow, and we could both go along with that and talk just as much as we liked. It is foolish really – as long as you appear to be doing the correct thing, it doesn't matter what you actually do.

I suggested this to him, and he agreed.

"Until tomorrow, then," he said, and bowed low, before running back down the corridor.

I can't wait!

OCTOBER 21, 1589

I'm the most miserable person in the whole
world. I hate Queen Elizabeth. She's ruined
everything. I could be flogged for saying that,
but at present I do not care.

This morning, she woke up in a filthy mood.
She was shouting and screeching at everybody.
First it was the maid who positioned her wig –
"It's not straight, you ignorant hussy, do it
again." Then it was the courtier who arrived to
tell her news from France who met with her
anger – "I don't believe a word of what my
lying spies tell me, they are in the pay of
the French King".

She reduced Letty to tears by telling her she came from a line of no-good upstarts who couldn't tell a chest of gold pieces from a sack of dung. And only because poor Letty was telling Grace about a letter from her mother which said they had had some bad luck on their estate! She can be monstrous sometimes.

But worse was to come, for me anyway. About ten, the Queen suddenly decided she wanted to go to her palace at Nonesuch. Not a word of warning to anybody in advance, no time to get anything packed. She said she wanted peace and quiet for a few days, but of course not too much, so all her ladies-in-waiting had to go with her.

I took all my courage in both hands and asked if I might be excused because I had made an engagement with an old friend. Well, you'd think I had asked her to give me the crown of England. "Ungrateful, turncoat, upstart, rebel, unnatural –" those were just a few of the words she called me. How dare I put another person's wishes before the Queen of England, how dare I defy her…

I managed to leave a message for Will, explaining what had happened and saying we could meet again in a few days' time. Then we rode off to Nonesuch, me cursing silently all the way.

OCTOBER 25, 1589
BACK AT GREENWICH

This is a copy of a note I found waiting for me when I got back today.

My dearest Mistress Swann,

I was very disappointed not to see you the other day. However, I understand the situation. The hunt turned out very fortunately for me. I was introduced to the Earl of Essex, who is going to fight in France to help the French King. He has taken me into his body of fighting men, and we are to leave immediately.

It seems that once again we are fated to meet only for a few minutes. When I return, however, nothing – and nobody – will stop me from bettering our friendship.

This is a great opportunity for me, and in a way I owe it to you. I will not forget that – or you.

With deepest regards,

Will Devine (who may yet be Sir Will)

FEBRUARY 14, 1590: WESTMINSTER

Today was the first day I have enjoyed myself
since meeting – or rather not meeting – Will. It
has been absolutely freezing here, and the River
Thames has completely frozen over. A special
Frost Fair was being held on it to mark this
unusual event, so we all went down to see what
was happening.

It was marvellous. There were traders selling
delicacies, furs, exotic spices and meats. I bought
myself a fur muff to keep my hands warm and
Frances bought some spiced sweets, which were
delicious. We had hot wine flavoured with
cinnamon and lemon peel to keep us warm.

There were some jugglers who were using lit
torches to juggle with, and a group of
mummers, who were skating on the ice.
We sat on bales of hay to keep off the cold and
watched them for half an hour, and it was very
fine. They were so funny, always falling down
and crashing into each other. I haven't laughed
so much since Lady Fitzwilliam's pet monkey

The Frost Fair

bit Lord Danbury on the backside!

In the evening, we watched a special performance of the play *Doctor Faustus*, by the writer Christopher Marlowe. It told the story of a man who sold his soul to the devil. It was frightening, but sad also. Sometimes I wish I was a boy so that I could be an actor. I know what my mother would say if she heard me saying that – all actors are worse than thieves and should be locked up. She still thinks that acting is a sin, even though all the courtiers enjoy watching plays. I love it.

Afterwards, there was dancing, as usual. I was standing talking to Frances and Letty when a man who I had never seen before came up and asked me to dance.

I didn't understand what he was saying at first, because he had a very strong French accent. He was about thirty, quite tall, with a very long blonde moustache and hair cut to just below his ears.

The dance began. Luckily it was a gentle pavane and not the energetic volta, because I didn't feel like leaping around. The French man said, "Madame, I am Pierre Deschamps, from Normandy. I noticed you today at the Fair. You are Mademoiselle Swann, no?"

"Yes," I answered.

"Well, I must tell you that I think you are very beautiful, Mademoiselle. I hope we can get to know each other some more."

I didn't know what to say. I just smiled and

carried on dancing, and rather hoped the music would hurry up and come to an end.

But when it did, he wouldn't let me go. He insisted on dancing the next two dances with me. I must say, he was a very good dancer. He swept me round the room and never took his eyes off me once.

He was full of compliments for me, and the court, and the Queen. In fact he seemed to love everything about his surroundings. He was charming, but – oh, I don't know. I'm just not used to French ways, I suppose.

I was slightly relieved when the Queen announced she was tired and wished to go to bed. I could truthfully say that I had to go and attend to her.

Deschamps gave me a sweeping bow, and gripped my hand very tightly. "I 'ope to speak with you again, Mademoiselle Swann. Perhaps I could escort you and your friend to the Fair tomorrow."

I hesitated, trying to think of a good reason why not. "Well ..."

He obviously thought I was just being coy. "Fantastique. Then I shall be at court at ten. Good night."

And with that he left the room, nodding at people he knew as he passed them. I noticed as he walked away that he had a slight limp. I wondered idly how he managed to dance for so long.

I joined Frances. "Fran, who was he?" I asked

her, because she's good at keeping up with who's who at court.

"He's a well-connected gentleman and a merchant," she replied, with a big smile on her face. "He's a Catholic of course, but I heard he was very charming, and full of compliments for English ladies. He's obviously taken a fancy to you, Rebecca!"

I suppose I should be flattered. But for some reason, I'm not. I could never marry someone like him. He's too smoothly spoken and eager to flatter. He's nothing like Will – oh, I didn't mean to write that. Will is just a friend. That's all he can ever be. My duty is to marry a rich man. And Deschamps is rich. No, no, no! I won't!

FEBRUARY 19, 1590

In the past few days, wherever I go, Deschamps keeps popping up. After Frances and I went to the Fair with him, he seems to have considered me to be his best friend. He's sent me posies of flowers, some sweets, even a ribbon for my hair.

He's very interested in the English court. He says he finds Queen Elizabeth fascinating. He asks me all about what sort of life I have here, what I do for the Queen, what she is like, her habits – in fact, thinking about it, he almost asks more about her than he does about me. I hope I haven't spoken out of turn about the Queen. He is a very persuasive questioner. I must be more guarded in future.

MARCH 3, 1590: GREENWICH

Deschamps has been out of town for the past week and I have to say it's been a relief. He's gone off to Oxford to visit an important earl there. After we arrived at Greenwich yesterday, I had a little note from him saying he would be back by the end of March. He said Oxford was charming. I also received flowers. That is the third bunch this week. Frances still thinks I should be pleased. She keeps telling me how wealthy he is. I don't care, although I know my mother would be overjoyed. I haven't written to my mother about this suitor.

For all the flowers and compliments he gives, something feels wrong. It's not just that I'm not interested in him in that way – I don't trust him. But I don't know why.

MARCH 8, 1590

I went to London today, to visit Catherine. She had her first child in February and wasn't ready to see anyone before now, but she sent her servant down to escort me there today.

I was riding through Southwark towards Tower Bridge, following the manservant, when I happened to notice a man on horseback. Nothing unusual about that, I know. Despite the cold, there were lots of travellers on the street. It would be fairer to say I noticed the horse. About two weeks ago, the Queen and a group from court went out hunting. Frances and I were part of the group, and Deschamps came too. He was riding the same horse then that was on the road in front of me now.

I'm not a naturally suspicious person. I never know about the secrets that get whispered around court until Frances tells me. But my mind certainly started working hard this time.

Why was somebody riding Deschamps' horse when he had gone to Oxford on horseback? I knew that for a fact; I had asked him myself if he was going by coach and he said no. Who was riding that horse?

I peered carefully at the rider in front of me. He was heavily wrapped up, but it was a cold day. I was covered in a cloak and a heavy hood, and I doubted if my own mother would have spotted me from three paces away.

The rider pulled up in front of a run-down house and dismounted. A servant came hurrying out and led the horse around to the rear of the house. This man was obviously expected by the occupant of the house. He limped up to the front door, climbed the steps and knocked.

The limp gave it away immediately. I remembered watching him leave the court room the first night I met him. It was Monsieur Deschamps! But I had had that note only yesterday addressed from Oxford. This was very strange.

A woman, quite shabbily dressed, answered the door. She had dark hair and a very worried look in her blue eyes. There was something familiar about her. Deschamps said something to her. I couldn't hear the words but the tone was sharp.

The woman's eyes filled with tears and she started to cry. And that was when I recognised her. It was Lady Anna Holdenby, the woman who had been banished from court the day I arrived. She stood back, drying her eyes, and let Deschamps in.

Something odd is going on here. I don't know what yet. But I'm going to find out.

MARCH 9, 1590

I've spent the whole day trying to find out more about Lady Holdenby. It's difficult getting information about someone without people wanting to know why. However, I know a little more now.

She is the granddaughter of a courtier who was a very good friend of Sir Thomas More, Henry the Eighth's Lord Chancellor. It is complicated. I had to get Frances to explain some bits to me.

When Henry wanted to marry Anne Boleyn, Queen Elizabeth's mother, he tried to get his marriage to his first wife, Katherine of Aragon, annulled. The Pope refused to grant him this wish, so he broke his allegiance to the Pope and with Catholicism too. He declared himself to be head of the church in England.

Henry passed a law saying that everyone if asked must swear that he was the supreme head of the church in England. That is why the Lord Chancellor, Sir Thomas More, was executed. He refused to take the oath, because he was a committed Catholic. Lady Anna's grandfather was a staunch Catholic too and also refused to take it. He was executed a short time after Thomas More.

Apparently, people were surprised when Anna came to court to be a lady-in-waiting because of all this. However, her father, who is dead now, was a good lawyer and had served the Queen well in her early years on the throne.

After Lady Holdenby was banished, her husband was released from prison and they left London and went to live in the north. He died of smallpox shortly after. Nobody knew any more about her after that. Some people even think she's dead.

She's very much alive, however. I know two things. She obviously doesn't have much money to live on. And she is afraid of Deschamps. But why?

MARCH 10, 1590

Oh dear me, what a day. I'll never trust another Frenchman for as long as I live. Let me tell you what happened.

I could only think of one way to find out what was happening with Deschamps and Lady Holdenby – to go and ask. As simple as that.

I went to Lady Holdenby's house first thing this morning. I broke all the unwritten rules of the court and slipped out without any escort whatsoever. When I got near to her house, I stabled Star at an inn. I didn't want Deschamps dropping by and seeing my horse outside the door.

I checked the back of the house, but there was no sign of his horse. Lady Holdenby answered the door to my knock.

Her hand shook as it held the door open. I got straight to the point. "Lady Holdenby, you don't know me, but I need to talk to you urgently. May I come in?" I asked.

She looked intently at me for what felt like a

lifetime. I must have a trustworthy face, because she let me in without a word.

When we were seated in the cold withdrawing-room, she studied the floor. I didn't waste any time.

"My lady, I saw Monsieur Deschamps calling at this house yesterday. I am an acquaintance of his, and I know he is supposed to be in Oxford. I also know you are very frightened of him." Now she did look up. "Why? What's going on? Something isn't right, I know it isn't."

Again, I received a long stare. Then without any noise or fuss, she began weeping. Three times I had seen her, and each time she was crying.

"I'm sorry," she whispered. "I'm so sorry."

"Why? What are you sorry for?"

"For – " she paused. "For what's going to happen."

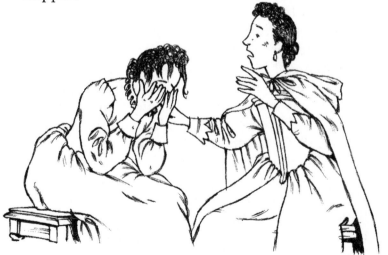

I felt like screaming at her. "Please, my lady, what is going to happen? Is it something to do with Deschamps?"

She nodded. "He's going to poison the Queen – tonight."

I shot to my feet. "Poison her!" I screeched. "How do you know? Why? When? How?" I demanded. "And why are you involved?"

"He blackmailed me," she said, faintly. "He's a spy for the Spanish, and he found out I was a recusant – "

"A what?" I asked.

"A recusant. Somebody who still follows the Catholic religion. I go to Mass secretly. That is where he found me. He said if I didn't do what he told me, he would inform the Queen that I was a traitor. He said – he said with my family history, I would be executed."

"So you're helping him to poison the Queen of England?" I asked angrily.

"No!" she answered, with more life in her voice. "I didn't know about that. I would never have helped him. I thought he was smuggling goods. He said he needed to use my house for storage and to meet people. I only found out yesterday. I overheard him talking in the other room. I thought I should do something but I didn't know what." She got up and started pacing the floor, wringing her hands together. Her voice rose. "I'm banned from court and I have no transport to get there. It doesn't matter now though. I'll hang anyway. I'll hang. They will execute me."

I thought she was about to start screaming so I leapt up and grabbed her hands in mine. "No, Anna, you won't. Not if you help me stop him. I'm going to take you to court and you must tell them everything you have heard. It's not too late."

As we left the house, it all made sense to me now. This was why Deschamps had made friends with me, to get information about the Queen. How much had I helped him? I wondered.

The Queen has summoned me. I'll finish this later.

MARCH 10 – MIDNIGHT

I'm a heroine, a star child, a lucky charm! The Queen has promised to give me anything I desire. Those were her words to me this afternoon. I shall have to remember that. But I must record the rest of today's events.

The hours after we left Anna's house were a whirl of action. Poor Star was forced to gallop non-stop to Greenwich carrying the two of us on his back. When we got there, I dragged Anna behind me all the way through the court to the one person I knew could help me.

Francis Walsingham, the Queen's principal secretary, is also head of the secret service, of her spies. Nobody mentions it, but the whole court knows.

When I arrived panting at his chambers, I burst in without so much as a knock. He was sitting behind his desk, and barely moved a muscle at my noisy entrance.

"Mistress Swann," he said, as if we were old friends. I'd never spoken to him before. But he knows the names of every single person in court. That's his job.

"Sir Francis, forgive me the intrusion but there's no time for being polite. There's a plot against the Queen. Pierre Deschamps will try to poison her tonight. Tell him, Anna."

She said clearly and simply, "He plans to poison her bedclothes. There's somebody here, a maid, I don't know who, who is helping him," she said.

Sir Francis had still not moved. "Wait here," he ordered. "I want to know everything when I return." With that he swept out of the room.

64

When he came back, I told him everything. About Deschamps asking all those questions about the Queen. About the horse, about seeing Deschamps at Lady Holdenby's door, watching him frighten her – everything.

Anna told him her story without any hesitation. She did not say one word in her defence. But I did. I made him promise that she would be taken care of and not punished for her crime. The look of relief on her face was enormous.

Just as I was leaving his office, Sir Francis said to me, "Mistress Swann, when things like this happen, we try to keep them quiet, so that the court and the common people don't panic. But I feel I can speak on their behalf. England owes you a great debt. Thanks to you, our beloved Queen is safe once again."

"What will happen to Deschamps, sir?"

"He will get his just reward," he answered. There was a grim look on his face. I didn't dare ask anything else. But I feel certain that no one will see him again. People who threaten the Queen of England do not die quietly in their beds of old age. And if he had succeeded in wooing me, I would have met the same fate – a terrible thought.

Anna is to leave for Pembrokeshire tomorrow at Sir Francis' suggestion. I hope life will be kinder to her than it has been so far.

JUNE 1, 1591: RICHMOND

The events of last year now seem like a dream.
I heard through Sir Francis that Lady Holdenby
has married a gentleman farmer in Wales and is
expecting her first child. I am so glad for her.

The Queen decided in the spring that for the
first time in about seven years, she is going to
go on a tour of the countryside this summer. So,
of course, the whole court has gone mad once
again with plans, correspondence with country
lords to decide where the Queen will stay, new
clothes, transport – honestly, it's chaos. But I am
as excited as the next person. I haven't seen
anything of the countryside of England apart
from my home territory in Gloucestershire. I
don't think the route of the progress, as people
call it, has been decided yet, but I hope it is a
long one!

JUNE 5, 1591

We have completed our first day's travel. We are
heading west, and will go as far as Bristol. Oh, it
is such fun! We are moving very slowly, because
of the massive number of people who are
travelling together. There are about forty
courtiers, their assistants and servants, who
make up another forty easily, the cart drivers and
horse masters and the Queen's personal
attendants. Then there is a troupe of entertainers,
plus cooks and general servants. We are like a
small army. And occasionally we get some
travellers on the road who join up with our
procession, or wellwishers from the small towns
we pass through walk alongside us for a few
miles.

We are stopping tonight at a house in
Berkshire which belongs to a brother of one of
the courtiers. He and his whole family have
moved out and are staying with neighbours to
allow the Queen and some of us to stay there –
me included, thankfully. There are some
advantages to having to wait on the Queen
sometimes. It means you can never be quartered
too far from her, so you usually get better
sleeping conditions. There are still eight of us
sharing one room though. Frances and I are
sharing a bed. Just imagine though – I could
have been lumbered with Lady Constance,
who snores like a pig so I'm told.

JUNE 18, 1591

It has been one of the hottest weeks I can ever remember. We travelled every day for the first ten days, and I have to admit, I was exhausted by the end of it. Some of the places we have stayed have been awfully cramped. One night, six of us had to share one bed! It was quite big, but still! The Queen doesn't seem to get tired, but of course she gets a whole room to herself.

There is a lot of waiting around too. At every county and parish border, we are met by officials, who usually give speeches and hand out wine for toasts to the Queen.

Thankfully though, we arrived at Easthampstead House in Berkshire three days ago, and we are due to stay here for at least another week. Tomorrow night, a huge banquet is going to be held out in the garden and a pageant and acrobatic display organised by some of the local gentlemen. How glad I am that we don't have to organise anything for a change. No masques, no playing for the Queen – now she has a whole load of people eager to entertain her. She should go on these progresses more often.

AUGUST 1, 1591

I have seen the sea for the first time. It is only the Bristol Channel, but it is still seawater. We arrived in Bristol three days ago. We have had feasts with the Lord Mayor and more nobles than there are stars in the sky, it seems. I've given up trying to remember names. The number of people we have met during this progress is unbelievable.

I'm getting off the point. Frances's family have a house on the coast – as they are from Bath, it is not too far for them to travel – and we went to visit it today. The Queen did not wish to go herself but let Frances and me go with her parents "as a special treat to my special maids", she said. See how advantageous these progresses can be?

The Highwaters knew how eager I was to see the sea and ordered the carriage to go directly to the beach, even before we went to the house. Of all the sights I have seen these past few weeks, this was the best. It stretches on and on, never still for a moment. I remember when I was supposed to be meeting Will Devine that time, thinking it must be strange to be a sailor away at sea. I didn't like the idea. Now I envy them. Imagine sailing on and on until you spot land at the edge of the horizon. For the early sailors, who thought the world was flat and came to an edge that they might sail over, it must have been terrifying. How brave they were.

The Royal Progress

Will has still not returned from overseas. I heard through court gossip that after fighting in France he went to the Low Countries. I fear I shall never see him until we are both old and grey.

It makes me sad to think like this, so instead I shall think of happy things. Frances's mother has promised that tomorrow we can bathe in the sea. Some physicians say that sea bathing is good for the health. I predict that it will be very good for mine.

AUGUST 5, 1591

In these few days, I have learned to swim. It is so easy in the sea. It seems somehow to support you. The weather has been wonderful too. Oh, this has been a perfect holiday from everything. We are to rejoin the Queen tomorrow. It has been so refreshing to have a rest from the demands of serving her. Now I feel ready to face the weird and wonderful world of the court once again.

NOVEMBER 12, 1591: WESTMINSTER

The court is preparing for the yearly Accession Day celebrations on the 17th of this month. It will be thirty-three years since Elizabeth became Queen, after Mary died. It seems as if she has been the ruler of England and Wales for ever. For all that people still talk about how wrong it is for an unmarried woman to be Queen, I don't think anyone can imagine the country without her.

❧━━━━◅━━━━❧

On the subject of unmarried women, all the ones I know seem to be disappearing. Both Letty and Dotty got married in October, to two brothers, which is quite amusing. Letty is very happy, because she was in love with her husband-to-be, but I don't think Dotty is. She hoped to marry a childhood friend of hers, but her parents arranged this marriage because her husband has good prospects. He's pleasant, but not what Dotty would have chosen. She's better off than some girls though. At least he treats her well.

Frances thinks her parents are trying to arrange a match with a distant cousin of hers. She was engaged when she was about fifteen, but her future husband died, and she said no to somebody else. She said her parents won't make her marry anyone against her will, like some do. She has met her cousin a few times and is quite fond of him. I wish her well.

I try not to think about marriage. I remember when I came to court, I was so worried that I might have to marry immediately! But as time goes on, I think nobody will marry me because I don't have much money. Especially if they are poor, like me...

Anyway, I don't know if the Queen would even let me get married. Ever since the business with Deschamps, she has told me on quite a few occasions that I am her lucky charm and I am not to leave her. I have to play for her on all the evenings when she is not doing anything special, and she often asks me to put her jewellery or wig on her rather than one of her maids. It's nice to be in her good books, but the thought of doing this for ever! Each year that passes, the Queen becomes more demanding. Is it to be my fate to stay with her for ever?

NOVEMBER 17, 1591: ACCESSION DAY

The bells were ringing around the city from dawn onwards. The common people of London lined the streets to get a glimpse of the Queen as she went on a short tour of the city. It still amazes me how enthusiastic people are just to see her. I forget that they are not used to it. They yell and cheer and wave until you think their arms must ache. It was the same when we were on the progress this summer.

Queen Elizabeth just loves it all. I always think that that is when she is really in her element, showing herself off to her people. Her face, which is usually so pale and fierce, becomes rosy and she looks happier than usual. I suppose that's the best part of being a Queen really – receiving adoration from your subjects.

But the best part of the day for me was still to come. Oh, I've had such a wonderful time! In the afternoon, as usual on Accession Day, there was jousting in the tiltyard at Westminster Palace. I was sitting in the Royal Stand with Frances and most of the other ladies-in-waiting. The older male courtiers who were not going to be jousting were there too.

First of all, we had a display of acrobatics from a troupe who regularly perform for the Queen. Then there was an athletics contest. Some of the young courtiers ran against each other to see who was the fastest, and were in relay matches where they had to pass a painted stick between each other as they ran. It was hilarious when they dropped it. Then they held wrestling matches, and you could tell some of them were taking it very seriously. I think it was a good excuse for people to settle old scores, because of course no one is allowed to carry any weapons at court or fight on any other day.

Everybody was looking forward to the jousting tournament. The Earl of Cumberland was the centre of attention as the Queen's champion, because of course she can't joust herself. My father told me that my grandfather used to joust against King Henry the Eighth, before the King was knocked out for a few hours. Then the King gave it up.

◦━━▭▭▭▭▬◯◯▬▭▭▭━━◦

The Earl opened the tournament with a brief speech to the Queen. She gave him one of her jewelled gloves as a token, and he attached it to his suit of armour. It had a pattern of stars on it. Over it he wore a full-skirted cloak of blue lined with yellow. He had the usual heavy helmet on.

The action started. There was a long fence in the yard. The jousters stood at opposite ends of it, one on either side, and held their lances across their bodies. At a signal from the Chief Steward, they kicked their horses into action. The Queen's glove fluttered furiously as the Earl charged towards his opponent, the ground thundering beneath the horses' hooves. Everybody started shouting encouragement.

Clash! The lances made contact. The Earl's opponent, Sir Ralph, was a bit off centre with his aim and it brushed harmlessly off. But the Earl was spot on. His lance hit Sir Ralph smack in his midriff. The lance splintered almost to its middle. Everyone cheered madly. The Earl wasn't the Queen's champion for nothing!

The next two up were Lord Danbury and somebody whose armour I didn't recognise. The unknown jouster was dressed in plain armour but wore a dazzling red cloak over it. They bowed to the Queen, then began.

The unknown jouster set off at an amazing pace. He raced towards Lord Danbury. Clang! His lance hit Lord Danbury with such force that even though the lance splintered, the impact pushed Lord Danbury off his horse.

He hit the ground with an almighty thud. The crowd roared.

I think by the time the tournament was over every single knight had ridden against the mystery jouster. None could match him, not even the Queen's Champion, although he did better than most.

As the afternoon wore on, the whole crowd was buzzing with talk of the red knight, as most people called him. So was the Queen. She loves watching young men show off and compete for her attention.

Before the final run of the day, when lots of knights were lined up to joust in a group, the Queen called the red knight over to the Royal Stand. She untied a ribbon from her dress and secured it to the knight's armour, as a token. He bowed low. People muttered and whispered to one another – this was an honour indeed.

Then instead of getting back on his horse, the knight walked along the front of the stand and stopped in front of me. He didn't say anything, but put his hand out and waited.

I stared at the knight, hidden behind his visor, blushing to the roots of my hair. I could think of only one person who might ask me for a token. And he was overseas – wasn't he? Frances nudged me. "Well, go on," she hissed in my ear, "give him something."

I tugged one of my gloves off and handed it to him. He pinned it to his cloak with his cloakpin and bowed, before running slowly back to his horse.

The spray of mud and dust the dozen horses produced as they charged made it nearly impossible to see who had survived the run intact. But that bright red cloak was still in place, and on it my glove.

The red knight came trotting over to our stand as the crowd started to make their way into the palace. He halted his horse, and with his visor still down, said to me, "I find I do not want to give this back, madam. May I keep it a little longer?"

I knew that voice. "You may, sir," I answered, trying not to smile, "if I can see your face."

"But of course."

He pushed back his visor. Blue eyes looked out at me.

"Good day, Rebecca Swann," he said.

"Good day, Will Devine." And indeed it was!

JANUARY 7, 1592

Will has been at court since his Accession Day triumph. The Queen is very pleased to have another young, handsome courtier around her. But he has told me his funds are running low, and he must find a way of making a proper living soon, one that is more stable than sailing and trading from country to country.

It is so pleasant to have him at court. We have been out riding together most days, with others there too, of course. Every night at dinner, he keeps me enthralled with tales of the countries he has visited and the people he has met. He tells his stories so clearly, and without being boastful. And he makes me laugh so much. But – oh well. It's nice to be friends, I suppose.

Frances became engaged at Christmas, to her cousin, and is getting married in March. I'm pleased for her, but I'm also dreading it. She will be going back to live in Bath for most of the year, and I'm going to miss her terribly.

January 8, 1592

I've just had the strangest five minutes. Will came racing up to me and was behaving in the oddest way. He said he had had some great news, but that he had to go away for a few days and would tell me what it was when he got back. He couldn't keep still for a moment, and ran away almost immediately.

I wonder if he is going overseas again. He often says that his only real prospects seem to be abroad. It looks as if I am losing both my friends. I feel quite depressed with life. At this rate, I shall be left at court all on my own.

January 13, 1592

My hand is shaking so much I can hardly write. But I have to record this day properly.

Will came to find me this evening. He had just that minute got back from his mysterious journey. He asked me to go for a walk in the garden, and wouldn't take no for an answer.

"Mistress Swann," he began, as we walked through the Rose Garden, "I have had some wonderful fortune."

"I'm very pleased to hear it," I answered.

"You know I am an orphan," he continued. "However, I do have some family, but because of a family quarrel years ago, I never met them. But last week, suddenly, I received a letter from my uncle. He is a rich merchant who has an estate near Bath. He said that his only son had died of fever at Christmas. He said it was a punishment from God for leaving me alone after my parents died. He wanted to make amends to me and do the right thing before God."

Will paused for a moment and stole a glance at me. "Go on," I said.

"He is making me his heir. I rode straight down to see him at his home in Bath and it is all signed and sealed." Again he paused.

"I am delighted for you, Mr Devine. It is wonderful to hear of a friend receiving good fortune," I said.

"A friend? Yes, we are friends, aren't we? But – I didn't just go to Bath, Mistress. On the way back I went into Gloucestershire. To Huntsdon, in fact. I spoke to your father."

Now my heart started racing. "Wh- why did you do that?"

Will turned and faced me. "You know why, Rebecca. I asked him for permission to do what I'm about to do."

He took my hand and went down on one knee.

"I love you, Rebecca Swann, and I always have. Will you marry me?"

I thought my heart would break through my chest, so fast was it beating. But I didn't hesitate with my answer. "Yes," I told him, smiling, laughing and crying at the same time.

He got up swiftly, took me in his arms and kissed me. "I would have asked you long ago if I had had any prospects at all. Now that problem has vanished."

"Yes. But we've still got one problem," I said.

"What's that?"

"We've got to ask the Queen for her permission."

JANUARY 14, 1592

I didn't sleep a wink last night. I was the happiest girl in the world one moment and the most miserable the next.

What if Queen Elizabeth says no? I have to find out soon. I cannot wait. Tomorrow is Coronation Day. It's always a good idea to ask for things on celebration days. The Queen is in a much better mood than usual because of all the attention she gets.

Please God, let her say yes.

JANUARY 15, 1592: CORONATION DAY

We spoke to the Queen after dinner. All the usual feasting and spectacles went on throughout the day. I can honestly say I don't remember a moment of it.

The Queen was watching the mummers perform. I was sitting to one side of her, Will to the other. With my heart in my mouth I began.

"Your Majesty," I started. "May I speak to you for a moment?"

"Of course, my dear girl, my lucky charm. Speak away," she answered.

Now I had to be bold. "Do you remember you once promised me anything I wanted?"

"I do," she answered, slowly, cautiously. I caught my breath, but continued.

"I'd like to ask for it now, ma'am. I want your permission to marry Mr Devine."

"Marry, eh?" said Queen Elizabeth. She turned to Will. "And what, may I ask, do you propose to live on, Mr Devine?"

Will told her of his good fortune. "I see," she said, finally. "I did make Rebecca a promise, that is true. There is just one problem. I will only allow my lucky charm to marry a nobleman –"

Will and I looked at each other in horror. "But ma'am –" I started to say.

" – and therefore, Mr Devine, I am making you a knight. Kneel. Steward," she called loudly, "hand me my sword."

There was a sudden hush in the court room. Will dropped to his knees before the Queen, stunned. A steward appeared with the Queen's ceremonial sword. The Queen tapped him with it on both shoulders.

"Arise, Sir William. Now you may marry Rebecca. But be sure you bring her to see me. I desire her company frequently. Do not fail me."

"Yes, Your Majesty," he said, then grinned at me. "I always told you I'd be Sir Will, didn't I?"

But I was too overcome to answer him. After seven years, I'm going to be leaving the court. I'm a little sad and very happy all at the same time. I'll have a home of my own in Bath and I'll be near my best friend, Frances. I'll still come to court often.

But the best of all is this. The Queen has said yes and I'm getting married to my beloved Will. God bless Queen Elizabeth!

FACT FILE

THE TUDOR AGE

What do we mean when we talk about the Tudor age? It covers a period in history from 1485 to 1603 and the word comes from the surname of Henry Tudor, a Welshman who became King Henry VII. He defeated Richard III at the Battle of Bosworth to become the King of England and Wales.

QUEEN ELIZABETH I

Elizabeth Tudor was the daughter of **King Henry VIII** and his second wife, **Anne Boleyn**. She was born in 1533. In the same year, Henry declared himself to be head of the church of England, and declared that he didn't believe that the Pope was head of the Church. He also renounced the Catholic faith, for himself and his countrymen. Despite not being Henry VIII's hoped-for son, Elizabeth became the heir to the English throne. Her elder sister **Mary**, **Katherine of Aragon**'s daughter by the king, was stripped of her right, as eldest daughter, to become Queen when Henry VIII divorced Katherine. As she was seventeen years older than Elizabeth, you can imagine how fond she was of her new baby sister when this happened!

Henry VIII and his daughters

Katherine of Aragon — **Henry VIII** — **Anne Boleyn**

Mary — **Elizabeth**

But three years later, Anne Boleyn was beheaded and the King married again. His third wife, Jane Seymour, gave birth to a son, **Edward**, and it was Elizabeth's turn to be out of favour. As a boy, Edward automatically became the heir apparent, and Elizabeth was declared to be illegitimate. Henry VIII stated she should not have any right to the throne even if her brother died.

Mary was reinstated as the second choice after Edward.

When the King died in 1547, Edward became king at the age of ten. But he was never very strong, and after six years he died. Then Mary became Queen. She was very unpopular because she tried to make the country become Catholic again, and persecuted Protestants who resisted.

Mary died without having any children, and Elizabeth finally became Queen of England in 1558, when she was twenty-five. People in England were very pleased to see the end of Mary's reign. However, everybody expected Elizabeth to marry and hand over the running of the country to a husband. They were amazed when year after year went by and she did not marry.

Some of the people referred to in the book really existed. One of these was **Robert Dudley**, who became the Earl of Leicester. It was widely believed that he and Elizabeth were lovers – and even that he had his wife murdered so that he could marry the young Queen. However, they never married. Despite everything, Dudley wasn't of a noble enough rank to marry a Queen and perhaps Elizabeth feared giving away her power to a husband.

Some people thought she might marry **King Philip of Spain**, who had been married to her sister Mary. But Philip was Catholic, and Elizabeth was a Protestant who was committed to making England Protestant again. They were on good terms at the beginning of Elizabeth's reign, but eventually the two countries went to war and King Philip sent the Armada to invade England. The only other person who Elizabeth seriously considered marrying was **François, Duke of Alençon**, the younger brother of the King of France. This was when she was forty-five and he was twenty-five – perhaps not the best choice! In the end it came to nothing, and Elizabeth remained unmarried until her death in 1603.

James VI of Scotland, the son of Elizabeth's cousin **Mary, Queen of Scots**, was Elizabeth's successor. With his reign, the Tudor age came to an end and the **Stuart** era began. (His full name was James Stuart.) He united the crowns of England and Scotland, but it wasn't until a hundred years later that England and Scotland united politically and Britain as we know it today began to be formed. Queen Elizabeth was a remarkable woman in many ways. In an age when women were regarded as weak and inferior to men, she ruled England and Wales for forty-five years on her own and managed to defeat a much stronger nation (Spain) when it tried to invade. She was bright and intelligent and could speak at least four languages. She could also be extremely cruel and heartless to her friends and subjects. But under her, England became a real power in Europe and beyond. The Elizabethan era is often referred to as the Golden Age. Whether that is true or not, she stands out in history as a woman who challenged the accepted idea of what a woman's role in a male-dominated society was.

LADIES-IN-WAITING

Rebecca Swann would have been one of many girls who came to serve the Queen at court. It was looked upon as being a great opportunity for women (and men who became courtiers) to advance themselves and make money. The obvious way for women was to marry a rich husband, and this is what Rebecca's parents hoped would happen. Of course, lots of women were already wealthy and married and were more like friends to the Queen than attendants. Some were her own relatives. The ladies would play cards with her and gossip and advise her. They were some of the few people who saw her without her make-up and fine clothes. They weren't personal servants – she had more lowly maids to perform services like dressing her and bathing her.

Ladies-in-waiting were not paid, but they often made money by being granted favours, or sometimes by selling information about the Queen to foreign spies. Because they were close to the Queen, they might receive gifts or money from people who wanted the ladies to put in a good word for them with the Queen. As you can see from the book, the Queen had the power to say if her ladies-in-waiting or male courtiers could get married. Sometimes she didn't want them to do so because she didn't want to lose their services, or even because she was jealous, especially of young girls as she herself got older.

Religion in Tudor times

The church was far more important in the sixteenth century than it is now. It governed every part of people's lives. Until 1533, Britain, along with most of Europe, was Catholic, as it had been for over a thousand years. But times and ideas were changing. With the invention of the printing press in the previous century, written papers and particularly the Bible became much more widely available.

People began to question whether the Catholic faith was the only way to worship God. They resented the incredible wealth of the church, which produced rich bishops and abbots and poor common people. People who challenged the Pope and Catholicism were called Protestants. Some European states had rejected Catholicism by 1533.

Henry VIII's was a slightly different case. His main motive for destroying the Catholic church in Britain and introducing the Protestant religion instead, with himself as the head of it, was political. His first wife, Katherine of Aragon, had not produced any sons. She had given birth to a few infants, but they had died almost straight away. He wanted to divorce her and marry Anne Boleyn, his mistress, whom he believed would produce a male heir. But the Pope would not grant Henry a divorce. Henry tried to argue that his marriage to Katherine was invalid because she had previously been married to his elder brother Arthur, who had died. Under an old law, people were not supposed to marry their former brother- or sister-in-law.

The Pope did not agree, and Henry set up his own Protestant church.

Catholics in Britain were not allowed to practise their religion. People who did so were called recusants, and during some periods this was punishable by death. Henry executed Catholics, but he also executed some Protestants with strong beliefs who challenged his position. When Mary came to power, she tried to make Britain Catholic again, and led a strong campaign against Protestants. Thousands were executed, and people feared and hated her. Elizabeth herself was a Protestant, but while Mary was alive she had to pretend to be Catholic. When she became Queen, she converted England back to Protestantism, but her regime was much more liberal about Catholics (apart from a short period after the Spanish Armada tried to invade). She wanted peace in her kingdom, and had seen how persecuting people made Mary so unpopular a monarch.

THE COURT

A lot of references in the book are to the "court". You may think this means one particular building. But it doesn't. It means wherever the Queen and her courtiers (her ministers, advisors and ladies-in-waiting) were. Elizabeth had lots of palaces such as Greenwich, Whitehall in Westminster and Richmond; and houses such as Hatfield

The south of England and London

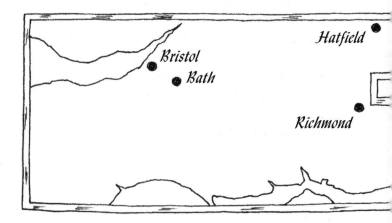

94

House in Middlesex where she spent much of her youth. When she moved around between her various palaces, her administrators went with her. Elizabeth had to move from palace to palace because they got dirty quite quickly and there was no way of coping with the waste produced by the court while it was living in one place.

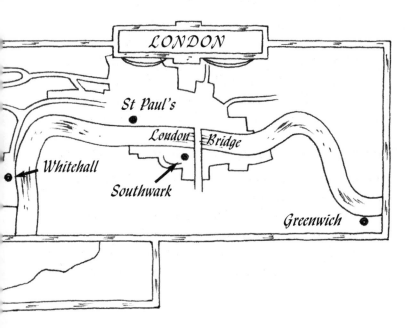

OTHER TITLES IN THIS SERIES

THE DIARY OF A YOUNG ROMAN SOLDIER

Young Marcus Gallo is travelling to Britain with his legion to help pacify the wild Celtic tribes. As the Romans march north, Marcus records in his diary how he copes with cold weather, falls in love and narrowly escapes serious injury. Read his diary and find out what life was *really* like for a young Roman soldier.

THE DIARY OF A VICTORIAN APPRENTICE

Young Samuel Cobbett is very excited – he is to be an apprentice at a factory making steam locomotives. Away from the shop floor, Samuel records in his diary how he learns his trade, falls in love and experiences accidents and danger. Read his diary and find out what life was *really* like for a Victorian apprentice.

THE DIARY OF A YOUNG NURSE IN WORLD WAR II

Young Jean Harris has just been hired to train as a nurse in a large London hospital. As Britain goes to war, Jean records in her diary how she copes with bandages and bedpans, falls in love and bravely faces the horrors of the Blitz. Read her diary and find out what life was *really* like for a young nurse on the Home Front in World War II.